A Coach's Letter To His Son

For Dan and Josh, who still make time to play ball with their dad. *M.A.*

Dedicated to the Seneca Falls Little League
for its assistance in creating the paintings for this book. *J.T.*

A Coach's Letter To His Son

by Mel Allen

PAINTINGS *by* John Thompson

CREATIVE EDITIONS

MANKATO

Text copyright © 2006 Mel Allen

Illustrations copyright © 2006 John Thompson

Published in 2006 by Creative Editions

123 South Broad Street, Mankato, MN 56001 USA

Creative Editions is an imprint of The Creative Company.

Edited by Aaron Frisch. Designed by Rita Marshall

Printed in Italy

Library of Congress Cataloging-in-Publication Data

Allen, Mel, 1946-

A coach's letter to his son / by Mel Allen; illustrated by John Thompson.

ISBN: 978-1-56846-134-2

1. Allen, Mel, 1946- 2. Baseball coaches—United States—Biography.

3. Fathers and sons. I. Thompson, John, 1940- II. Title.

GV865.A355A3 2006

796.357'092—dc22   [B]   2005052057

First edition 9 8 7 6 5 4 3 2 1

March 1

Keene, NH

Dear Dan,

The phone calls have started already, even though snow still covers the ballfield.

Parents are asking when I'll be starting baseball practice. Opening day of our youth

season is two months away, but they know I began practicing with you in a gym

before Christmas. They want me to work with their sons, too, to give them an edge.

It is all so different from how I learned the game.

When I was a boy of eight or nine living in a small Pennsylvania town, I spent my

summer days on a dirt baseball field near my house, standing on the far reaches of

the outfield, waiting to shag hard-hit balls that bounded past the fielders and the

trees before rolling into the thorn bushes. That was the early '50s, before Little

League and other organized sports for kids were formed. That was when older and

bigger kids ruled the sandlots. They wore no batting helmets, had no umpires, kept

score themselves, and, to the younger kids watching, seemed to play all day.

They knew my name and were not unkind, but I never played because I was too

young, too unskilled. Instead, I stood patiently in the tall grass, stepping into the

thorns a few times a day, then proudly winging the ball back to the fielders. When the games finally ended, I'd walk across the road to my house. At six o'clock, when two hours or more of daylight still remained, my father would come home.

We'd eat dinner, then he'd change his shoes and trousers and grab his baseball mitt—the one he'd had since long before the war—and we'd walk back across the road to the now-empty diamond. He was nearly fifty then, and he spent ten hours a day on his feet, but I do not remember him ever complaining when he sank into his catcher's crouch. I would wind up and throw, often bouncing the hard ball against his thighs and chest, or else throwing it beyond his reach, where it scuffed along the ground before hitting the backstop. I'd call myself Bobby Schantz or Robin Roberts, two Philadelphia pitching stars, and I'd pitch entire games, my father calling out balls and strikes.

I'd call myself

Bobby Schantz or

Robin Roberts,

two Philadelphia

pitching stars

ROBIN ROBERTS

In 1958, Little League came to town. We played the first games on Memorial Day, and we marched like peacocks in our bright new uniforms through the town, with bands playing and people lining the streets on the way to the field with the names of the local businesses painted on the wooden outfield fence. Parents sat on bleachers down the third-base line, and kids and dogs chased foul balls.

My father knew how tightly I held on to the dream of playing professional baseball on those summer evenings. And though he surely knew that would not happen, he never once told me so.

He died six years before you were born.

Late in the winter of 1986, when you were six months old, I took you to Winter

Haven, Florida, where the Boston Red Sox held their spring training. We were in a crowd just outside the entrance to the field, listening to the great Ted Williams explain hitting theories. He spotted you with the tiny red baseball cap pulled down over your eyes to protect you from the sun, and he reached over and plucked you from my arms and held you aloft. You were not afraid; you laughed and reached out to touch his face. He smiled and announced, "This boy will be a hitter."

When you were three, I videotaped you playing in the house with your aunt and uncle on Thanksgiving. I watched the tape again the other day for the first time in

We were in a

crowd…listening

to the great Ted

Williams explain

hitting theories

TED WILLIAMS

years. You are holding a tiny, yellow plastic bat, and your aunt and uncle and I are laughing at your wild, awkward swings as I toss you wiffle balls. Finally, you connect on one, and the ball hurtles towards the camera. You cry out in delight, and the tape shows you hitting one ball after another as we laugh along with you.

The following summer, I took you to a ballfield just up the road almost every day. I had bought you the smallest aluminum bat I could find, twenty-five inches long, and I rolled black tape three inches from the end to show you where to put your hands. I'd float baseballs to you underhanded, and you'd sail them over my head. One day, your great-uncle Robert came to visit from Philadelphia. He was eighty years old, and he sat in our backyard watching you hit. Suddenly, you launched a bullet across the yard, knocking the glasses off his face.

When you turned seven, we joined the local youth baseball league together; I signed on to be head coach. I had not seen you play ball with many other kids, but

after a few practices, I could see you were a special player. The other parents and

coaches did, too, and I heard their words of praise.

I bought my first book on coaching baseball, my first videotape on hitting. Our

play and practices blurred into one, and I was always free with advice I learned

from yet another tape or clinic.

I remember going to our ballfield one sun-filled Saturday when you were eight. I

carried a hundred baseballs in a large plastic crate. I had taught you to always step

towards the pitcher, but, as I pitched, I noticed you were stepping away towards

third base. I pointed this out.

"I'm not," you said.

"Yes," I said. "You are."

We argued and grew angry, and I started throwing faster, aiming for the outside

corners to show you that when you stepped away you could not reach my pitches.

You threw down the bat, and we drove home in silence. A few days later I saw that

you were no longer stepping away towards third, but we had ruptured something

less easily repaired than a hitting flaw.

By the time you were ten, you had attended three pitching camps and two hitting

clinics. Professional players showed you techniques that helped them make it to the

big leagues. There was always a waiting list to get in.

Your team has now won two city championships. Your All-Star team won the state championship last summer, then played in a tournament against teams from five other states. Trophies fill your room. When you are together with friends, you talk about what it will take to win the regional championship and go on to nationals.

After one game, an opposing coach came up to you. "I've watched you the whole tournament," he said. "You stick with it. You're going to be a good one." He turned to me and said, "Don't the good ones hit you like a bolt of lightning."

I was proud, though I tried not to show it.

I told you about Jon Matlack, the former All-Star pitcher for the New York Mets

I told you about

Jon Matlack, the

former All-Star

pitcher for the

New York Mets

JON MATLACK

and Texas Rangers, who grew up in my hometown. I told you that talent isn't

determined by geography; good players are found wherever they live.

During the winter, we throw twice a week in the school gym, and on Saturdays we

drive twenty miles to a set of indoor batting cages where twenty dollars rents a

pitching machine and cage for an hour. A college baseball coach, a part-owner of

the cages, watches you and offers suggestions. There's a video camera mounted

on a tripod nearby to capture your swing, so we can bring a tape home and dissect

your mechanics.

We arrive at the cage early before it gets crowded, and I invite a friend for you

because I am not sure you will go with just me anymore. I realized the other day,

after watching the tape of you at age three, then watching the tape we made at the

batting cage, that I haven't heard you laugh for a long time with a bat in your hands.

I have always loved the game. I have always wanted to go to a park with you in the

morning before the heat of the day and pitch a crate of balls to you and watch you

rifle line drives to the fences. I was surprised when I started writing this and real-

ized that I can't remember the last time you said you wanted to go hit or throw or

play catch. It has been me when once it was us. I wanted you to be the boy stand-

ing in the sandlot in 1954, wanting to play so much it hurt.

But you and your friends never had to want to play. We adults organized the

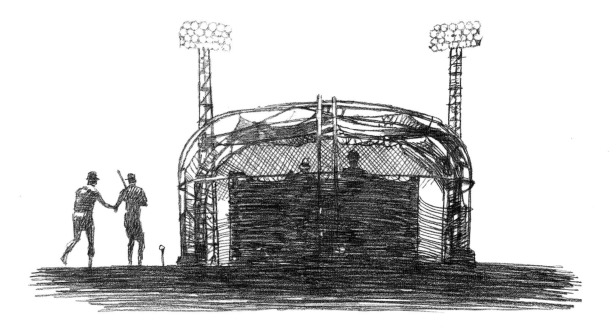

leagues and bought the uniforms and hired the umpires and formed the tournament teams and gave you trophies. Now you are twelve, and all that remains is to repeat what you have already done; anything less than winning a state championship you will regard as failure. Twelve years old.

I have pushed aside the countless times we have argued over baseball, a game which once seemed as light as blowing bubbles. Watching the tape we brought home from the batting cage, I see your face is taut, the face of someone who is chewing food he does not enjoy. You had not asked that a college coach stand three feet away and analyze your swing.

Sports are too hard to play unless they are played with joy. I write this to say to you that I want to start over. I want to put away the instructional tapes and the clinics and the winter talk about summer tournaments.

Sports are too

hard to play unless

they are played

with joy

ERNIE BANKS

I want to go to a ballfield early in the day and forget about finding the perfect form,

but instead find delight in putting all your strength and happiness into a swing. I

want to watch the ball soar before crashing into the grass and skipping past the trees

and into the bushes. And at the end of the morning, we can hunt for the balls, two

sunburned boys searching for treasure.